TEN MINUTE TALES

An Anthology of Poetry and Prose
written by the members of Ex-Cathedra,
a Norwich-based writing group

Shirley Buxton
Brenda Daggers
Lea Jamieson
Stuart McCarthy
Graham Porter
Avril Suddaby
and
Valerie Turner

SMOKEHOUSE PRESS, NORWICH.

First published in 2017
by Smokehouse Press
Norwich, NR1 4HB.

Typeset in Times New Roman
by Smokehouse Press.
www.smokehousepress.co.uk

Printed and bound by CMP (uk) Ltd.

ISBN 978-0-9576335-6-8

This book could never have been written and
produced without the inspiration of Joan, and we
dedicate it to her.

Ex Cathedra Writers would like to thank
Norfolk County Council Public Health and Library
Service for their valuable support and advice
throughout the development of this project.

Ex-Cathedra is also very grateful to
Peter Jamieson for his very kind permission to use his
work, *Cromer: East Beach, Windy Day*
as the cover illustration.

All proceeds from sales of *Ten Minute Tales*
will be donated to
the Alzheimer's Society.

CONTENTS

THE BEST OF RELATIONS

by Brenda Daggers

Olive stepped onto the train at Liverpool Street Station. Glancing around the deserted carriage, she sank down by a window and tucked her leather handbag and jacket on the empty seat beside her. As the train creaked into motion with a sigh, a chilly draught threatened to numb her feet. She hoped the stale reek of burgers and chips that permeated the carriage would not seep into her new cream cashmere jacket. Olive ran her fingers through her hair and stared at her reflection in the window, pleased she had taken up her hairdresser's suggestion of caramel highlights.

The crowded streets and high-rise buildings of London slipped past as the train gathered speed. Soon, small towns gave way to open flat fields of golden corn rippling in the breeze. Olive's thoughts turned to the last time she had made this journey to Suffolk. A shiver of excitement went through her, remembering herself as an excited child accompanying her parents on their annual holiday to visit the family in the coastal village of Barnley. How she had loved exchanging the grey concrete of their home in Clapham for the lush green countryside and beaches on the East Coast. Her Grandma and myriad aunties, uncles and cousins had all made such a fuss of her too. The very best thing had been sharing a bedroom with her cousin Jean. She would never forget the strange musty smell of that room that she could almost taste. In the bluish moonlight glimmering though the curtains, they would giggle together and gorge on midnight feasts of Grandma's chocolate cake. But that had all been more than half a century ago. The visits had petered out as she grew older and her life had moved on through grammar school, university, a career in teaching and her life in Hampstead with Pete and their two sons.

Over the years, news had filtered through of the marriages of various cousins and christenings when babies were born. Busy with her life in London, trying to balance her career and caring for her children, Barnley seemed a world away and Olive had all but forgotten the existence of her relations there. Then, just a few weeks ago, she had been amazed to receive a long chatty letter from Jean with an invite to a get together with the family. She had been even more surprised the way her heart had lifted at the thought of seeing them all again. Her husband's work often took him to Europe and both her sons had flown the nest and were busy with their own lives. Since that time there had been a permanent ache somewhere under her ribs, overlaid with ripples of envy when her friends spoke of their cosy, extended families.

On the tiny station in Barnley, a woman in a red fleece approached Olive, her arms held wide. She

3

enveloped Olive in a hug, grey hair scratchy like wire against her cheek.

'Hello. Remember me, Jean? I knew it was you straight away. Come on, all the family are waiting for you over there.'

Her cousin's rural tones transported Olive back half a century and she saw Jean with her fair pigtails plucking a sun warmed greengage from a tree in a long garden. Her heart sank a little when Jean waved her arm in the direction of a dingy restaurant, but she allowed herself to be pulled across the road and through the peeling brown doors.

Inside, so many faces looked up at Olive from the long table. Rosy cheeks, threadbare pullovers, broad smiles and hugs melted into a blur as they greeted her. She found herself seated before a plate piled high with pie and chips, although she had planned to eat a small salad, perhaps with smoked salmon or cottage cheese. Her relations introduced themselves, all talking at once. Auntie Maggie and Auntie Violet sat opposite Olive, both elderly ladies with walking sticks propped by their seats. Cousins Jean and Joan talked about their days spent pea picking in the fields whilst Uncle Fred and Cousin Roy joked about posh London ways. Olive concentrated on her pie thinking she must seem like a foreigner to them. But her pie was unexpectedly tasty and then Roy pushed a large frothing glass into her hand, beaming.

'Get that down you girl.'

Later, the sun dappled through the windows on empty plates. The excited chatter continued and Olive patted her bag thinking of the single ticket for the opera at Covent Garden for later that evening. She spoke over the hubbub,

'I should be getting back.'

'We're not letting go of you now,' Jean cried. 'We'll pick up my dogs from home and then we're all going for a walk on the beach. The oldies can sit and watch the boats.'

The sparkle of the sea was almost blinding against the blue sky. Olive slipped off her jacket and dropped it on a rock. Jean's two red setters dashed in and out of the water shaking salty droplets all over Olive. Jean threw a ball and the dogs flew after it, ears flapping, as it bounced across the sand. She linked her arm through Olive's.

'Do you remember Grandma used to bring us here to the beach. We used to build sandcastles near the water's edge, with a moat and a tunnel all the way through. My favourite part was when the tide came in and swirled all the way round.'

Olive laughed and nodded.

'And we used to make sand puddings on the top and stick those little paper flags on them. We searched for shells and put them in our buckets to take home. I remember the rock pools too, and us poking around in them looking for crabs.'

They passed other walkers who greeted Jean by name and stopped to chat. Olive thought of the silent spaces in her Hampstead house and the neighbours who never met her gaze.

Later, all the relatives came to see Olive off at the station. She rubbed her fingers over the ache under her ribs. She was so different, from another world. Surely they would not want to see her again. The rails began to vibrate and her train drew closer. Jean caught her hand.

'We're all off for a short break to Blackpool next month. Do say you'll come with us Olive dear.'

'I'd love to,' Olive called, waving as the train doors slid closed.

As the train headed towards London, she drifted into a doze, thinking, we are so different but they are the best of relations. She realised the ache under her ribs had vanished.

GONE IN TEN MINUTES

by Stuart McCarthy

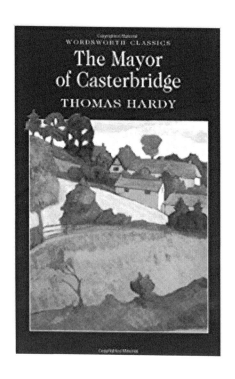

If my life was securely mapped out from early childhood then how was it possible for it to be completely derailed in ten minutes? That was how

9

long it took for me to see her and fall for her when our paths crossed in the café.

Let me explain. I was going to enter the Air Force as an officer. This had been decided by my parents from when I first showed an interest in aeroplanes. From that moment on they had guided my thoughts and actions towards the day when the letter from the selection panel arrived on our front door mat inviting me to attend selection at Biggin Hill. I knew I would not pass the tests for aircrew but my passion for engines and organisational ability made me a 'shoe in' for the engineering branch. That would mean a very happy life of postings to all different parts of the Commonwealth, attending ambassadorial parties, ordering people about, fixing aeroplanes when the pilots and navigators damaged them and generally having a good time. My rail warrant had arrived, was securely tucked into the pocket of my rucksack and I was all ready to go. My parents offered to take me to the station but I said that, as an act of independence, I would prefer to make my own way there. They were surprised but agreed and we said our goodbyes in the hall before I set off on my twenty minute walk to the station where my life changed course.

The smell of frying food assaulted my nostrils as I pushed my way through the door, sights set on a bacon roll. It was a small café just across the road from the station but with a reputation for doing the best breakfasts in town. There were no more than six tables and it was always full. Scanning the tables I saw there was just one seat left, on a small table right in the corner, and that the other seat was occupied by a slim, dark haired girl.

'Excuse me. Do you mind if I sit here?'

She looked up from her book, *The Mayor of Casterbridge*, and smiled. It was that smile that did it. Suddenly the café was lit from within with beams of sunlight, her grey eyes looked into mine and I fell.

'Not at all, as long as you don't mind me carrying on reading my book. I have almost finished it and want to find out the ending.'

'I could tell you, but I wouldn't want to spoil it for you.'

She looked at me, said nothing and returned to her book. Some ten minutes later she put it down and sighed.

'Sad ending isn't it?' I said.

She nodded and appeared to wipe a tear from her eye. I immediately offered her my handkerchief. She accepted it with a smile and offered her hand.

'Jane Plackett, pleased to meet you.'

'Brian Martin, likewise.'

'Do you like Hardy too?'

'Well I haven't read much of him. In fact just that one, but I enjoyed it very much.'

'Even the sad ending?'

'Well it seemed fitting, considering his actions.'

That sparked us off into a deep discussion on human motivation and we became so completely wrapped up in each other that an artillery barrage could have gone off in the street and we wouldn't have noticed it. What we did notice was that we were holding hands. Quite when that happened neither of us knew but neither of us wanted to pull away. Cups of tea followed cups of tea and the talk widened to shared interests, literature and music, and differences; I liked engines, she liked cooking. Eventually she asked, 'Where are you going today?'

'Biggin Hill.'

'Joining up?'

'Selection. You?'

'London, secretarial college.'

'Is that what you want?'

'Not now.'

Oh my God. She felt about me the same way I felt about her.

'Why?'

'Guess,' that smile and those eyes. 'You?'

'Same.'

'So what are you going to do?'

'Marry you.'

'That has my vote too. Parents?

'They'll go nuts.'

'I think they'll understand.'

Unfortunately, they didn't. They boycotted the registry office wedding and refused to talk to us for years. The ice finally thawed when our first child was born and the pull of grandchildren became too strong. When both sets of parents finally met they found common ground in their initial opposition and gratified surprise at our obvious happiness with each other and our family. By that time I was a successful businessman and Jane was a leading light in the Guide Movement. I kept on my passion for engines by financing a motor racing team and was able to treat father and father in law to days out at Silverstone and introductions to motor racing celebrities. They had 'come round' as I knew they would and we are now one happy and contented family.

For our fiftieth anniversary I took Jane to the café where we first met to give her a surprise present. A cup of tea, a bacon roll and a first edition of *The Mayor of Casterbridge*.

ALICE

by Avril Suddaby

All happy childhoods resemble one another, but each unhappy childhood is unhappy in its own way. Here are Alice Lock's memories of her childhood.

I wouldn't say that I had a happy childhood. Nobody can be blamed for that. It was wartime and everyone including children suffered in one way or another.

During the War I was living with my parents and my little brother in the East End of London on Hackney Road near the Children's Hospital. I can't say that I am a real Londoner as we came from Wolverhampton. My father was a footballer, he played for Wolves. But my brother really is a Cockney as he was born within sound of Bow Bells.

My parents had a sweet shop and we lived behind and over the shop It was completely different from how you'd buy sweets today. When someone wanted to buy sweets you weighed out the right quantity from the big jars and then put the sweets into a brown paper bag. There were no plastic bags then. We also sold ice cream. My dad made it following a family recipe which my grandfather got when he was in Italy. The ice was delivered to our shop and then we mixed the ice cream in big vats. It was hard work for my dad turning the churns for the ice cream but it kept him fit. My job was to serve the ice cream in little glass dishes and then to wash up the dishes afterwards.

The first way the War affected me was that it put an end to my schooling. I used to walk through Victoria Park to school with my little brother and after leaving him at his school, I'd go to my school next door. It was run by three elderly ladies and I think there were four classes. As soon as the War started the ladies closed down the school and moved away from London. Maybe it was sensible of them as soon a lot of the children were evacuated and there wouldn't have been enough pupils.

My mother didn't want her children to be evacuated. She always said, if we were going to die, it would be best if we all went together. I have clear memories of going to the bomb shelters. We went every night after shutting the shop, having our supper and leaving everything tidy. My mother was very particular about that. My father insisted on taking us to a different bomb shelter every night; he had some strange theory about it improving our chances of survival. The best of the shelters was under Selfridge's; they'd bring down lots of food for us and distribute it. And the worst was a tunnel under the river; that was cold and damp, with water dripping from the roof.

I remember my childhood as being very lonely. Most of my days were spent helping my mum in the sweet shop. I missed school and the other children terribly. I had loved school and enjoyed learning new things but the War meant the end of my education.

My best friend Pat wasn't evacuated so we saw one another as often as possible. Pat and I are still best friends and have been ever since we were five years old and first met at school. We still try to meet up once a year. When the weather was good enough we'd go for walks by the canal and when it was bad, we'd go to each other's houses. Pat didn't like coming to my home because my mother always found jobs for us to do. My mum was a bit like that, always organising people and bossing them around. So more often I'd go to Pat's.

Pat's dad was an undertaker. The dead bodies were stored in a big shed at the back of their house until they were taken away to be buried. The four black horses and the hearse were kept next door in a stable in the archway under the railway. You've probably heard of the tragedy which happened at the Bethnal Green bomb shelter where a lot of women and children died as they were trampled on when people panicked. Pat's dad never recovered from the horror of that and they say he was never the same man afterwards. There were more bodies than he could cope with and he had to call on his brother and uncle to come in and help. They were undertakers too, it was a big family business. Pat's mum was responsible for the financial side. I remember her collecting the subs every week. East Enders believed in grand funerals and spent many years of their lives paying in advance for a good send-off.

Sometimes I'd go to the baker's over the road. He was a German Jew and his brother came over from Germany at the start of the War. The brother was very artistic and I'd help him with all sorts of painting. We'd make signs for the different shops, labels for the sweet jars, whatever needed doing.

Many of our neighbours were Jews. Everyone has heard of Cable Street, which is just round the corner from Hackney Road where we lived. The Mosleyites used to come smashing the windows of the Jewish shops. Tempelsky's the tailor's was just opposite us. Once when they were smashing up the Jewish shops they broke our shop window. I suppose our name, which was Blanco, didn't sound like a good English name. My father went after them asking why the heck they'd broken our window when we weren't even Jewish. Mosley got to hear about it and insisted his men came to replace our shop window.

Yes, I remember seeing Mosley. He was very tall, dark and good-looking with lovely manners. I think my mum fancied him. Anyhow when his men came with the new glass my dad remonstrated with them. I'm not having that, he said, I want plate glass like we had before. And Mosley was a perfect gentleman. He made his men take the glass away and put in plate glass. Of course the Jewish neighbours didn't get the same treatment. I remember my dad saying to Tempelsky, why don't you just rub out the "sky" at the end of your sign, then no one will know you're Jewish. They must have eventually done what he suggested because Tempels Gentlemen's Tailors is still in business. But for most of the Jewish shopkeepers it was just a fact of life, a hazard like the bombs, and they'd just get on with repairing their shops and back to work. A few weeks after Mosley repaired our shop window it was blown out by a nearby bomb. We did eventually have a direct hit which demolished the back of our house. Our dad found a flat for us in Maida Vale but he'd come back every day to see to his shop.

Towards the end of the war my dad was called up. When we got the papers my mum didn't believe it. I'm not letting them take you, she said. She thought it was a mistake because he was too old. But it turned out to be no mistake. He was sent to Kettering where he learned how to mend shoes. Ever after I had to wear shoes with big thick soles after my dad had mended them. He was one of the last ones to be called up.

These are some of my memories of my childhood. It was not like the lives of children today and I'm glad of that.

THE SCOTTISH AFFAIR

by Shirley Buxton

Harry had been living alone now for seven years. Since Mollie's death, he had continued living in the same house with the same visitors and the same daily routine. Harry tenderly recalled the wonderful years he had enjoyed with his wife. He smiled as he remembered Mollie's great love for all her family and friends. The couple's warm welcome and generosity of spirit, ensured people wanted to keep in touch with them. Years on and the steady stream of visitors continued to knock on his door.

For many years Harry and Mollie had hired a residential beach hut on the coast. They had joined their children at play, delighting in the simplicity of sand and sea. During their holiday week they were always joined by various family visitors who looked forward to their day on the beach with Harry and Mollie. These gatherings, together with Christmas, held so many precious moments. Still times were moving on. He was gathering new family memories as grandchildren married and he became a great-grandfather.

Harry contemplated the elements of his routine that had changed. His weekly outings now always included a Saturday visit to the 'Bookies'. Often on his way back from his 'flutter' on the horses, Harry would pause to look into the Travel Agent's window. It ignited recollections of past holidays. If Mollie had been here, she would be pointing out interesting places. They would have wondered about going somewhere different, maybe even abroad, but then probably would have settled on going to the guesthouse they'd been to many times before. Those holidays were in the past. 'It isn't too late to do something different,' he told himself.

One life-changing day, Harry opened the door of the Travel Agent and stepped inside. His eyes moved across the shelves. Colourful photos of sun drenched beaches glossed across the cover of brochures advertising breaks in foreign climes. Harry hadn't stepped out of England since he was demobbed after the war. To go abroad at his age seemed one step too far. 'Explore the British Isles by Coach.' Now that might be more his mark. His eyes were drawn to a full page photograph of purple heather clad hills rising up from a peaceful loch. The autumn colours of silver birch together with graceful firs were reflected in the waters. Majestic mountains in the distance rose up to meet a clear blue sky. In the foreground, a friendly hotel issued a warm welcome. He thought of Mollie.

Less than two months later Harry was standing on the front steps of that very hotel drinking in the magnificent Scottish scenery. It was every bit as amazing as had been portrayed in the photo. The week refreshed him, revitalised him, and made him feel so much younger than his eighty seven years. He knew this feeling. It was the one he had when he met Mollie and that which came when each of his children had been born. It was the feeling of rich, deep love. When he had first touched Mollie, gently caressing the curves and hollows of her body, he'd been thrilled and excited. He'd thought of the experience as exploring a virgin land, his hand passing over gentle hills and lush valleys and he'd felt alive.

The following year Harry booked himself onto four Scottish tours, eager to see his new love clad in the different seasons. The rushing of the spring waters and fresh growth gave way to a maturity of summer. The glories of autumn colour and clear skies were transformed into a winter wonderland by the first snows. Harry was surprised by her differing moods. He became keen to know her better. The number of times he climbed onto the Scotland coach increased year by year. He would book up different tours, but he always favoured his first love. In most months he would say goodbye to East Anglia for a week, anxious to be enfolded in the embrace of his beloved Scotland. With passing years, his love deepened.

Family members quizzed him about the people he'd met and friends teased that he'd found a lady friend. Sometimes he would play along, alluding to his 'new mistress.' Christmas cards arrived from fellow travellers. The coach drivers and couriers joked that he knew all the tours so well he could easily take over their role. They'd pass him the microphone, encouraging him to share his knowledge and love of the lochs and glens.

Harry had plenty to talk about to his visitors back at home. His life was full. He had found happiness and contentment. Moving away from where he had been born never crossed his mind. His roots and family were in Norfolk and that was where he belonged. One might say that Harry's relationship with Scotland was really just 'an affair', but for Harry it was a deep love that filled him once more with life.

A CAT'S LIFE

by Shirley Buxton

Born a whisker from death
      Tiny torso licked into life,
      A mew of existence.
Suckled deep in Tabby fur,
      Paddle breasts for creamy flow,
      Snuggled sleep in warming purr.
Siblings scuffle, paws of four,
      Wriggling forms, blindly explore,
      Held in safe haven of mother.
Eyes open to a world beyond,
      Senses heightened, smells abound,
      Harsh sounds causing fright and flight.

Climbing, tumbling, chasing, hiding,
  Scrapping, nipping, kittens play,
  Milk-full mother ever watchful.
Tasty titbits, rough tongues lapping
  Bold adventures brought to check,
  Gentle strokes and soft held neck.
Snatched from kitten innocence,
  Cat alone in foreign home,
  Welcomes human comfort.
Chasing papers, perching high,
  Curious cat courts disaster,
  Exploits evoke mirth and chidings.
Butterflies invite paw play,
  Then poised to pounce, hidden, still,
  Bloodied feathers; the first kill.
Her season heralds fresh affections,
  Tom-cat odours on Tabby fur,
  Courtship sounds pierce cold night air.
Rooftop walks, impregnation,
  Expectant waiting, instinctive preparation,
  Birthing calmly, quiet in secret,
Expertly cleaning, warming, feeding,
  Her babies clambering for attention,
  Mother, exhausted rests content.

A WALK IN THE PARK

by Brenda Daggers

LONDON EARLY NINETEEN FIFTIES

His eyes seemed to follow her as she hurried down the stairs, pulling on her gloves. The photograph of her father, standing erect and unsmiling in his army uniform seemed to dominate the wall. Below it, was the photo taken over a decade ago of herself and her sister Rose, diminutive girls with pigtails and wearing

31

matching white fluffy boleros. Behind them, stood their brothers Frank and George, their usually unruly dark hair combed flat.

Rose was waiting for her in the hallway at the bottom of the stairs, wearing a navy two-piece with white piping around the jacket. She called up to Margaret, 'Come on. Let's get our Sunday walk over with. Father, Frank and George are waiting outside for us.'

Margaret buttoned up her coat and the sisters linked arms.

Their father stood, with Frank and George, outside by the square lawn. When his daughters emerged through the front door, he pulled his watch from his waistcoat. Its loop of gold chain dangled, glinting as he pointed at the dial, frowning. They all trooped along behind their father to the park.

Margaret and Rose trudged along at the rear, following the usual twisting pathway between the trees. Margaret looked at Rose. Even stumbling along in the mud and rain, her sister somehow managed to look beautiful. Her lovely heart shaped face glowed with health and she had pinned a red flower in her chestnut curls which always looked as though they had been polished. Margaret felt her own mouse brown hair coming loose from the knot at the back of her neck, and rain dripping from the trees in cold rivulets down her neck. She knew how she must look with her narrow face, nose turning purple and hair plastered to her head. She turned up her collar. A hidden tree root tripped her and she sank to her knees.

Rose hauled her up, 'Look at you. Those stockings are ruined now.'

Margaret's shoulders slumped. She thought how good it would be to sit at home listening to the wireless and crocheting the chair back she had just begun. But there was always so much to do with all the cooking and washing and ironing and cleaning.

'I've been looking after everyone for years since mum died in that air raid. I'm almost eighteen, but Father never lets me go anywhere. It feels as though my life will never change. At least you get out to your job in the hat shop.'

Rose tucked damp strands of hair behind her sister's ears.

'You're too kind Margaret. You let him walk all over you. It isn't right.'

'But he needs someone to look after him, and Frank and George too.'

As they plodded on, Margaret thought about how other girls her age had proper jobs and went out enjoying themselves. Then, her breath caught in her throat. Charlie. It had been two years since they had danced all evening under the chandeliers at the Flamingo Dance Palace. Since then, she thought about him every single day. Remembered his arms holding her to him, her face pressed against his jacket with its damp wool smell as they said goodbye outside at the end of the evening. His lips warm on hers so that she forgot the chill of the night. He must have forgotten about her long ago, maybe even married someone else. Sometimes she cried at night in the room she shared with Rose.

Rose giggled and nudged her making Margaret jump. 'I've got an idea. It's time we had some fun. '

Margaret laughed, feeling guilty at the same time. As well as the loss of his wife, they all knew their father hadn't been the same since coming back from the war. More than once, when cleaning the upstairs hallway, she had seen him crouched down by the tallboy in his bedroom. Heard him mumbling about shells all around him.

Rose seized Margaret's sleeve and inclined her face towards her sister's ear.

'Next time Father, Frank and George have an evening playing cards, I'll keep topping up their glasses with beer. They'll be fast asleep in no time. Then we'll catch the tram up to Hackney High Street and have ourselves some fun at the Flamingo Dance Palace.'

Margaret's pale grey eyes widened. 'Ooh Rosie. You wouldn't dare. Suppose Father wakes up and finds out? What if he needs me?'

Rose grinned at Margaret. 'It will be fine. Leave it to me.' As they walked along the muddy path, the rain eased and sunshine broke through the clouds.

In the bedroom that evening Margaret fluffed up her hair in front of the dressing table mirror. She promised herself she would brush it every night so that one day it might shine like her sister's. A shiver of excitement ran through her. In just two days they really were going to sneak out and go dancing. Reflected behind her she could just see the battered edge of Rose's tan suitcase poking out from behind the chair in the corner. She couldn't stop staring at it. Rose had said she mustn't look inside. She was making preparations and they were to be a surprise.

It was Saturday evening at last. Margaret had hardly slept the night before. Closing the door to their bedroom, Rose dragged the suitcase across the floor and heaved it onto her bed.

'Father's fast asleep, his false teeth in the glass by his bed. I had a quiet word with Frank and George to keep an eye on things.' Now, close your eyes Margaret. It's time for your surprise.'

Margaret closed her eyes. She heard a faint rustle. When Rose told her she could look, a gasp escaped her lips. Rose was holding up the prettiest dress she had ever seen.

'I've been sewing this for you in my breaks at work. We get sample fabrics for the hats and they let me have this for next to nothing. It's real parachute silk. Come on, get your pinny off and that old grey thing you're wearing and try this on.'

When Margaret had peeled off her apron and dress, Rose slipped the new dress over her head. She gasped at the sight of herself in the mirror. The cherry red silk flowed over her thin frame, warm yet cool at the same time against her skin. The glass beads decorating the bodice glimmered with a pale iridescence. As she turned before the mirror, the skirt, billowed out around her knees. She stroked her arms, so pink and bare. What would people think?

Rose rummaged in the suitcase again. 'Now for the finishing touches. Stand still.'

Margaret stood whilst Rose brushed her hair around a band decorated with silk flowers. Next came a sparkly bracelet and matching necklace. Margaret's stomach flipped over when Rose rouged her cheeks and applied bright red lipstick to her lips. Rose hugged her.

'Perfect. My beautiful sister. Now I'll get ready and we'll be off.'

On the tram to Hackney, Rose and Margaret talked about the new styles. Rose said she could give Margaret a home perm. Margaret was shocked. 'But what would Father say?'

When they entered the tall doors of the Flamingo Dance Palace, Margaret forgot all about Father, all about her worry that her dress wasn't right, all about her sadness.

Inside the dance hall, the walls and ceiling were bathed in a yellow glow. The band were playing the new Frank Sinatra, 'I've Got You Under My Skin.' Rose disappeared amid the crowds. Couples danced past Margaret as she sat at an empty table, some gazing into each other's eyes. Suddenly, she felt very alone. A movement on the far side of the hall caught her eye. Margaret pushed her way through the couples on the dance floor and stood behind a pillar, her heart pounding.

Charlie was sitting with his back to her. Next to him was a woman. A beautiful woman wearing a silver dress. Margaret made to turn away. Charlie had a fiancée or a wife now. Of course he had forgotten her. She heard her name called. Saw the woman whirl away on the dance floor with another man. Charlie stood before her smiling, his arms held wide.

'My own dear Margaret. I always knew I'd find you again one day.'

Charlie led her onto the dance floor. As they danced to the strains of 'You Belong To Me' Margaret knew that after tonight her life would be changed forever.

AN ENCOUNTER

by Lea Jamieson

It was in the early 70's, a late evening in May. I was in the Naval Nursing Service using my skills in Plymouth. The next day I was due to have my exit interview with the Chief Medical Officer and later in the week to go on to Malta as a midwife.

I settled happily into bed after reading and turned out the light. Suddenly it felt cold. I drew up the meagre sheet and blankets around me wondering at the unexpected chill. No matter, it would be warm in Malta.

Closing my eyes I expected sleep to come, but instead I felt strangely alert as if someone was watching me. I resisted the sensation and snuggled deeper into bed, but the feeling persisted. Reluctantly I opened my eyes to the darkened room and saw a figure! He was standing to the right of my bed in front of the wardrobe. A scream entered the space between us and my hand reached out to put on the bedside light. The scream sounded strangely puny in the silence and my body froze into the bed. I was caught in the gaze of this man of no substance and yet clearly seen. He looked directly at me with eyes piercingly sad. He was dressed in clothes of another time, with white stockings, cream breeches and a white dress shirt with a sort of frill at the throat. His pale thin hands held a tricorn hat. It was similar to my nursing outdoor hat but more ornate. I gazed transfixed at him and he at me. In the now lit room, he started to disappear from the feet upwards. It was slow like one of those childhood magic toys that you drew on and then slowly pulled a tab and the image disappeared. There was no hurry, just a steady revealing of the wardrobe behind. The last part to go was his face. I can still see the pallid skin and powerful eyes.

I was left sitting up in bed with the covers tight around me. I did not believe in ghosts and the figure had challenged my comfortable view. I was silent with amazement but my mind was racing with thoughts. Who could he be? Would he come back? I was relieved my exit interview was tomorrow and I would leave by the end of the week. I would have to sleep with the light on. Would anyone believe me? Would I have believed anyone? I doubted it. I didn't believe in ghosts. But I did then. Fear and confusion speeded my thoughts. I stayed alert with the light on till the morning sun filled the room, and then I fell unaware into an exhausted sleep.

The next morning I felt silly and unwilling to share what had happened. At breakfast in the officers' mess there was talk of a scream. I said I had woken in a nightmare. I could not speak of my experience. It felt so contrary to the breakfast chatter.

The activities of the day brought a sense of calm. With some trepidation, I went to the Captain's Office to receive my report and papers for Malta. It felt rather like standing outside the Headmistress's Office at school. I had not been before and found the Administration was in a very old building, the corridor walls were wood panelled and hung with oil portraits of past captains. I stood outside the door waiting to go in and my mind returned unbidden to the ghost's face full of desolation. I knocked dot on time, assuring myself this was a mere formality, and

43

advanced to a curt, 'Enter,' The Captain looked up and after a moment invited me to sit; I sat but could not concentrate on what he was saying. Behind him hung a full length portrait of a naval officer. He was wearing a uniform jacket now covering his shirt and his hat was on. I think he held a sword but I only saw the pale hand which I knew I had seen before and from his face the same eyes looked out straight and cold. They did not have the sadness but it was him.

The Captain asked me if I was all right. I answered trying to smile, 'I'm fine thank you, Sir.' I tried to concentrate on his voice to distract me from the picture and the fear that rose in me. The interview over I left, a silent groan seemed to quiver through my mind, no memory of the Captain's good wishes just an overwhelming knowledge that my ghost had existed in the flesh, and I had to sleep in my room again tonight.

GIRLS AT LARGE

by Valerie Turner

On either side of the platform steamed two trains, and between them two young women with their parents, still smarting from unwelcome news that the War Office was parting them as land girls: Jean was destined for Norfolk and Daphne for Devon. They rolled their eyes as their parents sniffed; 'Make sure you keep safe.' and 'No messing about with boys.'

'One suitcase Daph?'

'Yes my uniform, underwear and a dance dress.'

Jean gave a wry smile. 'Somehow, I don't think we shall be so lucky.'

'Hurry up young ladies,' shouted the guard. Hastily they hugged, promised to write and before they knew it, each was on her way to 'do their bit'.

Daphne arrived at Axminster in darkness, to be met by a taciturn farmer, who had been waiting several hours for the slow moving train. She was 'welcomed' with a plate of stale bread sandwiches before being shown the room in which three other girls were sleeping. She stripped to her underwear and dived under the thin blankets to cry quietly.

Jean made it to Norwich just in time to hail the last taxi, which took her miles further into the countryside. She thought of her friend as the taxi drew into the farmyard. A sliver of yellowing light guided her to the door, and a woman's voice called, 'Come in girl, you must be frozen.' A bowl of hot soup and bread rolls were thrust across the table as a large man entered the dreary room.

46

Immediately, her hostess said, 'We are Mr and Mrs Bennington. Eat up and I'll show you to your room.'

'It was my son's bedroom,' Mrs Bennington said later. 'He was killed at Dunkirk.'

'I'm sorry.'

'Don't be . . . it was war.'

Chastened, Jean fell silent, overcome with tiredness.

'Breakfast is at six, out in the fields by seven.' The woman's gaze fell upon the girl's manicured hands. 'Soon be calloused and scratched like mine', she prophesised.

Jean nodded dumbly as the woman left her. 'Oh Mum, why didn't I go into the forces?'

She was woken by a continuous humming sound at first light. What was it? Neither a horse nor a lowing cow; and a loud cockerel had only just begun his shrill crowing. So what was that continuous hum? Shivering, she splashed icy water on her face and hands, hurriedly donned the uniform green jumper, brown breeches, socks and lace-up shoes to present herself downstairs.

'Sit yourself down girl,' growled Mr Bennington, who was heaving himself into a khaki overcoat. 'Across the yard is the cow-shed and piggery with the horses nearby. Mother will tell you where I'm to be found.' And he left.

'Work hard and you'll find he's quite an old softie.' whispered his wife.

Hm, thought Jean, not believing it, and made her way across the yard. It was a fair-sized farm she was discovering, with extensive outbuildings, and sheep and goats in the nearby field. In the cow byre she found three men milking.

'Don't just stand there; you will be doing this tomorrow'. Her heart sank. She was beginning to understand that there was more to the countryside than pretty fields and flowers.

'Sit you down here girl, aside of me.' A fresh-faced, smiling boy of about sixteen was pulling forward another stool, 'Now girl . . . '

'My name is Jean.'

'That's nice; I'm Ken. Now g . . . Jean, watch me pull and squeeze, see? Twice more and it's your turn.'

That evening, she sat at the table, writing. Mr Bennington faced her, adding up columns of figures biting on his pipe, while his wife darned a sock by the miserable fire.

Dear Mummy and Daddy

Already, I am missing you; it is so quiet here. Well, except for the American B17s that warm up at five o'clock every morning on the airfield which isn't far away. Today, I learned to milk a cow, and tomorrow I may ride on the tractor taking the churns to the Pickup Point, wherever that may be. I hope you are both well. Mr and Mrs Bennington are very kind. I guess I shall soon get used to it all?

Your loving daughter,

Jean.

'Mother!' Mr Bennington whispered hoarsely, seeing that the girl's head had drooped.

'Oh!' his wife laid the sock aside and gently shook the sleepy girl. 'Come you along my dear, up the wooden hill.'

The insistent hum of the bombers warming up at the airfield woke her again in the dark dawn. She shivered; she had not undressed last night! Oh, and it was almost six! She stumbled down the uneven staircase to find Mrs Bennington alone at the table; her tired face was drained of colour.

'Been up all night dear, with Bessie.'

'Who is Bessie?' asked Jean.

'Bessie? One of the cows, she's calving. When you have eaten, would you take Mr Bennington a Thermos of tea for me?'

A single light bulb swung gently from the end byre, and a low groan led Jean to the gate, where her steps in the straw were heard by the bent figure raising the creature's tail.

'Is that you Mother? Take the end of the rope will you?' The man had turned and his expression of annoyance told Jean that she was the last person he needed to help. She put down the Thermos and stepped carefully towards the cow, and the man and the rope. He sighed loudly. She noticed that he had thrown his coat over a nail, and how his chest rose and fell with exertion.

'You are a city girl, too skinny for this,' he grunted, but she gritted her teeth, closed her eyes and pulled on the rope as though her life depended upon it. Sweat trickled down from his brow as he barked, '1, 2, 3, heave! And again Jeanie.' Her breath came in short bursts as, yet again he ordered; '1, 2, 3, pull Jeanie! Come on Bessie, nearly there . . . one more push . . . ' The poor creature protested loudly.

'Jeanie, don't stop, pull girl; you are doing fine! Yes, yes, here comes . . . come along my little darling.' He grasped the calf's first leg, as another followed by two more while Jean stood, head bowed with exhaustion and exultation, the rope limp in her hand. She glanced up at the man wiping his hands as he approached her.

'Isn't nature wonderful? You don't see this in Birmingham little woman.'

51

He ushered her over to the milking shed where in a low voice, he said: 'You are doing well Jeanie. You are a fast learner; so fast, I think you should learn to use the plough.'

She quaked at the thought, yet by the end of the week, when she realised she had never worked so hard in all her life, she had never been so happy.

She and Mrs B as she had come to call her, were bottling fruit one afternoon after 'sticking' for fuel from the woods, and checking the sheep in the lower pasture. She looked down.

'My hands are hideously worn, Mrs B. you were right,' she said as she looked down, and together they laughed.

In her next letter to Daphne, who had not yet written to her, she wrote,

Each day is different. I hope you are as happy in your place as I am here. Last Saturday, I went to a dance in the village hall with Ken and his sister. Mr B took us there and back by tractor! By the time I had cocoa with Mrs B regaling her with news of the latest songs and dance steps, it was midnight, and the cows would still have to be milked at seven. Oh, I do hope you are getting on well?

Write soon,

Jean x

It was on Saturday morning when they were making plans for the Harvest Supper that the postman brought her a short reply from Daphne.

Dear Jean,

I am glad you are getting on so well. The four of us were treated badly by our 'employers': little food, no baths, and a 16 hour day . . . dreadful. So much so, that we took the train to Dartmouth, and are now training to be Wrens in the Royal Navy, where life is good. When will this wicked war end?

Fond love,

Daphne x

'Bad news?' Mrs B put an arm around her, seeing a teardrop on the letter. 'Are you happy dear? It's a hard life, working on the land. I hope you are not too tired?'

'No, Mrs B. I'm packing the vegetable boxes for the Harvest Festival tomorrow.'

'Leave room for my four loaves of bread please. I am still cross about those pears I was going to give. They were coming along nicely. I didn't go to the orchard for about a fortnight, and when I did? No decent pears to be seen. The birds must have scavenged them.'

It was during the second hymn, when children took their gifts to the altar, the next morning that Jean nudged Mrs B. and the woman whispered, 'Well I never, the scavengers!'

Angelically, three children proffered their ill-gotten pears, and avoided Mrs. Bennington's glare as they walked back to their seats.

Afterwards, while the farmers talked together and their wives were brought up to date with all the village news, Jean slowly walked ahead.

'Jean!' called Mrs B. excitedly. 'There are two more land girls hereabouts. We shall have to get you introduced.'

Jean smiled to herself. When would they ever meet, working a sixty-hour week for the princely sum of two pounds? Ah! The scavengers were in her sights. She would have a word with those rascals.

She quickened her steps, and at only a few paces behind them, thought of Daphne: a smarter uniform and salary maybe, but she would never change places with her friend, because from her perspective, life would never be dull for a land girl.

2.30 FROM LIVERPOOL

by Stuart McCarthy

What would he miss most, he asked himself as he sat at the table in the crowded station buffet. Well he wouldn't miss the coffee they served here for one. He would miss the company of books though, that and the chance to read and understand the minds of great writers. But they would soon be behind him and he would be off to somewhere where there would be no more pain, no more humiliation and no more despair.

He sipped at his coffee making each drop last an eternity until his train arrived. He tried to imagine the reactions of people at home and work when they heard of what he had done. He tried to think of a phrase to describe their reactions and 'total indifference' was the best he could come up with. Yes, 'total indifference' described it perfectly, his parents, his boss, his brother all would say something like, 'Typical, never a thought for others.' Well that was why he was going to do it; to not be a burden to others. They had never cared for him at all. They had always told him he was stupid, missed the point, had no common sense and always left a job half done. They criticised him for his choice of employment and his inability to get a girlfriend. His brother was always held up as a paragon, as one to be emulated. If only he wasn't so stupid. He couldn't be the lawyer who earned millions like his sibling, instead he worked in a grotty little bookshop for the minimum wage. It was all he was fit for and such disgrace to the family. Furthermore, his brother had strings of doting girlfriends and he, not one. His father was convinced he was gay which was an even greater disgrace. No, they wouldn't miss him.

He lifted the cup to his mouth and drained the final dregs. He had ten minutes until his train. The sun, streaming in through the buffet windows threw everything into stark relief. He was suddenly very aware of his surroundings.

'You're sad,' said a child's voice in front of him. He looked and saw a helmet of black hair draped over a pair of staring eyes and a nose resting on the surface of the table. The rest of the face and the child were hidden below the table top.

'No I'm not,' he said, 'I'm very happy.'

'Then why are you frowning?'

'Because I feel like it.'

'Why?'

'Because I might miss my train.'

'Why?'

'Because I am sitting here talking to you.'

That stopped the questioning for a moment, just time for the next set to be considered and delivered.

'Which train are you getting?'

'The 2.30 from Liverpool.'

The face vanished and he saw the small child it belonged to scuttling away to the timetable on the wall. She, for it was a girl, consulted it with great gravity before whizzing back to resume her position.

'There isn't one,' she said, 'I know, we learned to read timetables at school. And there isn't a 2.30 train from Liverpool.'

'Well it comes through here and I'm getting it.'

'But it doesn't stop.'

'It will for me.'

'Do you own the railway?'

He smiled, something he hadn't done in weeks, and shook his head.

'No I don't.'

'Then why will it stop for you?'

'Shannon, don't be so nosey,' the voice was female, adult and very harassed. The person it belonged to was a head shorter than him, he judged, with long black hair framing an oval face. The eyes were soft and kind and the smile was warm and friendly.

'I am so sorry,' she said, 'she's always talking to strangers and annoying them.'

'That's all right, she wasn't annoying me.'

'Can we sit here mummy?' asked Shannon in a plaintive voice.

'No dear, the gentleman doesn't want to be disturbed and he probably has a train to catch.'

'No you are welcome to sit here; I have to be going in a few minutes anyway.'

'He's going to catch a train that doesn't stop here.'

'No I am sure that's not true Shannon.'

'But it is, mummy, he told me he was going to get the 2.30 from Liverpool and it doesn't stop here. I know, I looked.'

'Perhaps you made a mistake dear.'

Shannon disappeared from the table, dashed across the floor; reread the timetable and dashed back.

'No I didn't mummy. There isn't a 2.30 from Liverpool. But he said he can make it stop for him.'

'I am sure he didn't say that dear.'

'But he did, and may I go to the toilet?'

'Yes, but be quick.'

'And will you be here when I get back? I like you.' Shannon reached out her hand and touched his, the first tender human contact he had had for years.

'Yes,' he said, 'I'll be here. Just make sure it's before half past.'

Shannon gave him a beautiful smile and raced off.

'Why?' the mother asked.

'Why what?'

'Why are you doing this? Catching a train that doesn't stop. Doesn't take a genius to work out what you are going to do. I just wonder why.'

'Because my life is a mess, no one likes me, I am a failure and it would be better for everyone if I wasn't here and in seven minutes I won't be. There, now you have it. Does that satisfy you?'

'Doesn't give me much time then.'

'To do what?'

'To convince you to stop this madness and give life another chance.'

'Why should you want to do that?'

'Because Shannon likes you, and I like you.'

'You've only just met me, you know nothing about me and I know nothing about you.'

'OK, a quick six minute rundown on Linda Chapman, that's me by the way. I am twenty three years old, had Shannon when I was sixteen, her father wanted nothing to do with us and my family threw me out. I lived in hostels and refuges for three years. Then I got a job in a second hand record shop with a flat above. I live there. I manage the place now, and am hoping to buy it. Shannon is always looking out for a dad but has never taken to anyone as quickly as she took to you. I think she sees a kindred spirit in you, and so do I. I would like you to come and help me run my shop and you can live with us in the flat. And there is a spare room before you ask. I can offer you a fresh start, and I think it will be a very loving start. Well it will be on my part anyway. That's the offer, the decision is up to you.'

This was just too good to be true, there had to be some kind of catch.

'There is no catch,' said Linda as if reading his thoughts, 'and you have a very expressive face, it gives your thoughts away.'

She smiled and placed her hand over his. 'Give it a try and anyway, the 2.30 from Liverpool will always be here.'

He warmed to her touch and knew that he, Robert Tann, family idiot, failure and general disgrace, was falling in love.

'I'm back,' said Shannon resuming her place at the table. 'Is he coming with us mummy?'

'You'll have to ask him.'

The 2.30 express from Liverpool roared through the station.

'Yes,' he said, 'I think I am.'

SUMMER

by Lea Jamieson

Sea sparkles

Wet sand shines

Sandals scrunch on stones

Soggy sandwiches satisfy after a swim

Memories of laughter, wine and surf boards

Blue sky, bright beach balls thrown

Kites high, weaver fish warnings, tiny crabs found.

Punch and Judy rest beside sand sculptures.

The eternity of summer before school starts again.

Each memory dances at the sea's edge.

I sit content letting the sound of the softly surging sea
soothe deep within.

IT'S A HARD LIFE

by Graham Porter

Up the road in Melbourne, it's a bright spring morning. Down here by the water, the wind is arguing with the sunshine. My eyes watering in the breeze, I can just see across to the other side of St Kilda Bay. There, stick people lean forwards and battle the elements to earn their coffee in the kiosk that sits, invitingly, at the end of the pier. But I'm sitting with my back to the wind, hood up, enjoying the smell of the salty seaweed and the warmth of the spring sun on my face, and I'm counting my blessings. It's a hard life.

The seagulls are squabbling with the myna birds for tiny morsels on the sloping sand. Just offshore, a pelican patrols its own fishing ground with slow sweeps of its long beak. It tips its head back to swallow, then immerses it into the water once again, its whole neck disappearing for a few seconds each time. The wind whips the tops off the waves and white horses spin foam as far as the eye can see. Patches of grey-green cloud-shadow alternate with brighter areas where the sun picks out the sandy water in mustard yellow. The strong, steady sound of the wind in the palm trees along the shore is interrupted by the squawks of the mynas and the shouts of the skateboarders on their swooping track. On the smooth promenade, the downwind rush of a cyclist seems to mock the upwind struggle of a solitary jogger.

Coming towards me from the direction of the pier I can see a dark form. He is not 'battling' against the wind. He moves (and I think it is a 'he') with more of a shuffle than a walk and he stoops, rather than leans, into the wind. Eventually he makes it as far as the toilet block on the promenade. Reappearing after a few minutes, he continues his slow progress in a windward direction, and I realise that it won't be long before he reaches my end of the prom.

The wind steals the crest from another wave as it rushes towards the beach. My tranquillity is disturbed. Skateboarders, joggers, cyclists have all disappeared: there is only me and the weary man in the dark coat, plodding relentlessly along the promenade. The gap between us is closing and I realise I cannot just sit here and watch him approach. I swing my bag onto my shoulder and look around for my escape route. The path behind me leads to steps that will take me back to the road. He is less than two hundred metres away when I reach the steps, so that I can just make out his features. His fair hair is shoulder length but surprisingly well kept. I can see now that he is wearing a navy blue duffle coat that has most of its toggles missing. It's no surprise to see that his shoes are very worn. From a distance I'd have guessed him as more than sixty years old, but I judge he's perhaps more like fifty.

Is he on his way anywhere? Perhaps this promenade is his home. Does anyone else know, or care, if he lives or dies? All this I wonder without, I hope, appearing to stare. But now I have reached the steps, I descend towards the road and he is gone from view. I can no longer see him, but I have a feeling he'll remain with me for some days, along with the thought: it's a hard life.

ABDICATION

by Avril Suddaby

It was a time that I will never forget. The same subject was continually on everyone's lips and the papers were full of the latest news (or should I say gossip?) about the King. Of course, when it all started, he wasn't yet King; he was still the Prince of Wales.

He was a good-looking man and he had a way with people. What I mean is that he wasn't formal and correct like the rest of the royal family. He had played his part in the War, and there was no doubt about it: he was popular and wherever he went people came to see and cheer him. I never actually saw him myself but most days there would be photographs of him in the papers. Although I was not really interested in the rest of the news (I was a teenager then), I would look at my father's paper every day to see if there was a picture of Edward.

That's not to say there were no reservations about his affair with the American woman. At that time most people disapproved of divorce and she was already married to her second husband. After Edward met her (I think it was in 1930 when I was twelve years old), the papers soon realised that something was going on and pictures of them together started to appear, with never a sign of her poor husband. There were pictures of Edward and Wallis on the Riviera and other such glamorous places. She was a lovely looking woman, always tastefully dressed, always with a new piece of jewellery. I suppose Edward provided that for her. You could see from the photographs that he was completely besotted with her. As Edward was so popular, people tended to forgive what would have been unforgivable for most other men.

The newspapers and we, the common people, speculated about what would happen. It was said that Edward wanted to marry Wallis Simpson and that of course meant there would have to be a divorce. For Wallis a second divorce! It was said that his parents, and especially his mother, Queen Mary, were bitterly opposed to the marriage, and I imagine that most of the establishment disliked the idea of the future king of England marrying a divorced American woman.

Matters came to a head when the King, George V, died in 1936, about five or six years after the affair with Wallis had started. Edward then became Edward the Eighth, King of Great Britain, King of India, King of Australia, King of New Zealand, King of Canada,

King of Kenya, King of Nigeria, King of Burma, King of Malaya, King of Singapore, and King of thirty two other countries. But his passion for Wallis Simpson showed no sign of abating.

The press realised what was happening behind the closed doors of Buckingham Palace. There were frequent audiences with the Archbishop of Canterbury and the Prime Minister. From the grim expressions on the faces of Archbishop Lang and Prime Minister Baldwin as they left these meetings, it was easy to guess that the discussions did not go well. There were reports of interviews with other Members of Parliament. Most of them condemned the King's behaviour. A few, notably a young MP called Winston Churchill, spoke up in the King's favour.

And then the bombshell came. There was an official announcement that the King intended to marry Mrs Simpson and that she had asked her husband for a divorce. Edward's love for Wallis was so strong that he had said that he would rather renounce the throne than give up the woman he loved.

The establishment had to compromise if they wanted him to continue to be King and they were not willing to compromise. I think you can imagine the feelings of a romantic teenager, overhearing all the intense speculation about what would happen. I dreamt about finding a man who would love me as passionately and single-mindedly as Edward loved Wallis.

That evening I went with my mother and father to Buckingham Palace where a large crowd had gathered, although it was December and the weather was bitterly cold. The atmosphere was tense, fevered, near to hysteria; there were chants of 'We want Edward!' 'Long live Edward!' and even 'Long live Love'. Several people had made placards saying 'God Save the King from Baldwin' and 'We want our King'. If there were any dissenting voices they were not heard over the calls in support of Edward. I think we all hoped that the King would make an appearance on the balcony of the Palace but that didn't happen. Although I never actually saw the king, I will never forget that evening nor the preceding time of avid speculation about the future of England and her royal family.

The next day the King signed the papers of abdication, giving the throne to his brother Bertie who became King George VI. Edward had been king for less than a year. That evening, every single person in England sat huddled around their wirelesses, listening to Edward's farewell speech to the nation broadcast from Windsor Castle. He told them what they already knew: that he had abdicated in favour of his brother and explained why: that he could not live without the woman he loved. I believe that every woman and girl in England was in tears listening to his sombre words. After finishing the broadcast he left England, never to return. It had been an unforgettable year. The next year Edward married Wallis. They lived together in France for the rest of Edward's life and true to his words, he never was to return to England until after his death when his body was brought back to be buried at Windsor Castle.

LOTTERY

by Brenda Daggers

Rain drizzled on umbrellas. Elbows and bodies jostled against her as she strolled along the High Street. Kate was surprised that everything looked the same as it had yesterday. Before she had known. Somehow she had expected the street and shops and crowds to be lit with a golden glow. The automatic doors of the department store on the corner whooshed open with a sound like a sigh, swallowing her into the scented interior. Kate's feet made no sound as she walked through the makeup department, sniffing the scent of countless fragrances. Assistants in slim black skirts smiled at her, their hands poised, like alchemists, over rainbow arrays of tiny pots and tubes.

In the church-like hush of the beauty salon on the first floor, a young woman settled Kate into a squashy grey leather chair.

'I'm Chantelle and I'll be doing your beauty treatment today.'

Kate gripped the arms as her chair tipped suddenly backwards, startling her. She felt her slacks slide sideways across the seat and wished she had worn her favourite blue linen skirt. Really, she thought, this almost feels like being at the dentist.

Chantelle leaned over her, a halo of blonde spikes fanning out around her tanned face as she peered at Kate and her shiny purple mouth tightened as though someone had pulled up stitches around the edges.

'Now Kate, we need to sort out that muddy complexion. I can see you've not been keeping up with your cleansing and exfoliating routine. Those eyebrows have to go and I think, definitely, aquamarine frosted shadow to bring out the blue in your eyes. Then our new crimson berry lip gloss and you'll be a new woman.'

Kate's morning toast and marmalade seemed to be lying like a stone in her stomach. She didn't know what exfoliating was and she wasn't at all sure she wanted to be a new woman. It was all Sylvia's fault. Her friend had been ecstatic when she'd told her about winning the lottery money.

'That's a serious amount Kate. You must pamper yourself a bit. Celebrate. Have some fun. Take a holiday maybe.'

The trouble was, this didn't feel like fun at all. Chantelle was busy rubbing and tweaking her face, making her skin burn. When the mirror was thrust in front of her, a stranger stared back, a plastic doll with beige skin, red patches in its cheeks, pouting lips and spidery eyelashes against a shiny blue background.

Chantelle beamed. 'Lovely. You wouldn't know yourself would you?'

'Thanks very much.' Kate's voice had gone very small. She wondered what on earth   Philip, her husband, would think.

Chantelle pushed a tiny pink bag tied with a silver ribbon into her hand.

'You're very welcome. I've made you up a package of our products. We recommend all our customers make an appointment for a skin care special on a regular basis.'

Back home in her small house, Kate eased her feet into her frayed felt slippers and seated herself at her dressing table. Smoothing cold cream into her face she dabbed at her skin with cotton wool. She smiled as the old Kate began to reappear in the mirror, her skin clear and glowing; eyes blue and bright. Untying the silver ribbons of Chantelle's package of products, she stared at the tiny plastic tubes of foundation, orangey brown, beige and ivory. Drawn by the bright colours, she dipped her finger in miniature trays of eye shadow and smeared streaks of purple, gold and green on her eyelids. No, it wouldn't do. It didn't feel like her. The waste paper bin, heavy with holiday brochures, lolled against her right leg and she swept all the little pots and tubes in to join them with a sound like rain.

After cleansing her face once more, Kate made a pot of tea and carried it into the sitting room. Philip yawned as she pecked him on the cheek. 'Had a good day at the shops Kate?'

'Nothing special. Lamb chops for tea OK? Busy day tomorrow. It's my flower arranging class. Then I'm meeting Sylvia for coffee. Must remember to pop in on Mrs Gibley next door later, see whether she needs any shopping.'

Kate settled herself next to Philip and they sat in companionable silence, the only sound the click of her knitting needles. Philip's eyes drooped closed and his head nodded forwards. Kate gazed for a moment at the wedding photograph on the piano by the window. Her darling Philip, so tall and handsome in a suit; herself in a long white dress, a filmy veil like a cloud around her dark curls. How had the years passed so quickly? She smiled to herself. Yes, there had been ups and downs. Money was often short. Things had been hard when the children were young, but there had been so many good times and she knew she had been fortunate. Maybe they could think about getting away for a bit of a break in the Spring.

Phoebe jumped onto Kate's lap, kneading her claws in the fuzzy pink sleeve draped across her knees. Kate scratched the black and white fur behind her cat's ears and kissed the top of her head as she whispered,

'We're happy as we are, you, me and Philip aren't we?'

Disentangling Phoebe from the half finished pullover, Kate deposited her on the floor and tiptoed into the hallway. She lifted the telephone.

'Hello. Is that the Cat Rescue Home? I'd like to speak to someone about making a substantial donation.'

PATCHWORK TROUSERS

by Shirley Buxton

'What do you think?' Vicky held up a gaudy pair of patchwork dungarees.

'They were only fifteen pounds from Camden Market. The cheapest ones at Covent Garden were thirty. They'll go with absolutely everything!'

I waited with interest for her mother's reply.

'Sounds like a good buy Vic. They'll be great for the holidays.'

'Is my black T-shirt clean? It will show them off well when I go to orchestra tonight, or do you think red would look better?'

'Try them both and see what you think.'

Vicky disappeared to her bedroom, clutching her new purchase.

Colour co-ordination had never been our youngest daughter's strongest point. Perhaps this latest buy was her solution to this problem. I noted that Vicky had not pressed me for an opinion. This would be expected at her 'fashion parade', scheduled for when she'd solved the T-shirt dilemma. It gave me time to think up the witty response she would expect from her Dad. A straight comment of approval would be regarded as 'Dad's not interested,' while to show disapproval would be 'Dad's totally unreasonable and out of touch.'

I thought back to my own childhood. What would I have given when a schoolboy, not to wear patched trousers! One of my worst memories was starting secondary school. I had caught my brand new trousers on a protruding screw that held the tip-up seat of my desk. No thought in those days of the school admitting responsibility for the resulting tear. I was in trouble at school for not taking care of my appearance and in even more trouble at home where money was short and new clothes were a luxury. The greater punishment was not the thrashing I'd received but the shame of having to wear patched trousers. The material for the repair was taken from the side pocket, rending it useless. As I recall, pockets are of immense importance for an eleven-year old boy. The screw remained a daily hazard for the rest of that year in form 1A.

Patched and darned trousers were a common thing in our family. Mum spent most evenings mending, patching or knitting up reclaimed wool to keep us clothed and warm. The highlight each summer was when Cousin John came to stay. In addition to having a slightly older playmate for the week, there would be a large bag of clothes he'd outgrown, new clothes for me without the inherent dangers of newly bought items. I'd never been allowed jeans, but to my ten-year-old delight there in the bundle were John's favourite, well-worn jeans.

'Oh how did those old things get in there!' exclaimed my aunt. 'They were earmarked for the rag and bone man. Richard won't want those.'

'They'd be good for playing in the garden.' I quickly interjected.

'It would save his school clothes.' Mother agreed and so the jeans were mine.

What amazing memories those jeans held. The navy patch below the back pocket was from when John and I had been scrumping apples last year. There was now a brown patch on the other side.

'The result of an altercation with a large dog,' John had confided.

As well as two knee patches due to general wear and tear, there were the mends following his bike brakes failing on a down-hill whizz, as well as an incident involving a neighbour's fence. These jeans had a history that I was proud to inherit. Even before John returned home, I had added two more trophies, one the result of being snared on barbed wire and the other from rock climbing.

'Dad, what do you think?' I was jolted back to the present.

Vicky stood before me resplendent in a long sleeved purple top and her new dungarees.

'Stunning!' I flashed back. 'It conjures up memories of when I was young.'

'Dad?'

DOG WATCH

by Lea Jamieson

Eyes expectant hold mine
Body relaxed yet ready for action
Treat, walk or brush?
Anticipated enjoyment travels nose to tail.

Beach freedom is another learning
Room to move away explore and dig.
A sleek shaped canine distracts and
connection is broken in the excitement of pack
possibility.
They run and jump delighting in movement
Sharing a common interest of fur and fun.

Eyes watch the sky lightening with the winter sun
And marvel at the frost adding piquancy to play.

NINETEEN TWENTY TWO

by Valerie Turner

'There is a paucity of words in your vocabulary young Bertie,'said the baker, arms spread across the counter.

'A paucity?'

'Yes, you need education.'

'I've had it.'

'Some yes, but you don't want to be delivering my bread for the rest of your life, do you?'

'What do you suggest, Mr Merry?'

'I think,' said the large man, leaning over a tray of pastries, 'I think you should go to Canada.'

'Blooming 'eck Mr Merry, that's further than London.' He sprang back as the baker's fist thumped the counter.

'See? You are plain ignorant; your mother's dead God rest her soul, your father is a drunkard and he has six brats who are hooligans.'

'I'm not a hooligan Mr Merry, nor's my little sister, Florrie.'

'Nevertheless, I rest my case.'

'What case?'

Large brown eyes stared frighteningly long on Bertie. 'Before this year is out, Canada will have taken enough 'stalwart peasants.''

'What's stalwart? I am not a peasant, Mr Merry.'

The baker sighed, 'Take these pastries Bertie and on your way back call into the Council Offices where they are crying out for ignorant peasants like you.'

'I am not … '

'Just go . . . enlist . . . and when you get to Canada you can change your mind . . . see? Scoot!'

At last Bertie was at the table, before two burly be-whiskered men. 'Next . . . name?'

'B . . . ,' clunk! The man behind him had dropped something. Bertie bent to retrieve a sleek, black fountain pen and handed it to him.

'Thank you.'

Not 'ta', but 'thank you', thought Bertie, he was no peasant either. He collected himself at the impatient tapping of a pencil. 'Name?'

'Bertie Smith aged 17.'

The two men conferred. 'Sure about that?'

'According to my family's calculations; my mother's dead and Pa is ill.'

'Hmm . . . a wastrel no doubt.' The men whispered again. Bertie was looking out of the window as the man asked, 'Where do you live?' And out of the lad's mouth popped the name of the street opposite. 'Sandringham.'

The men's glances met, eyebrows raised. 'Really?' asked one and 'Have you met the King?' enquired the second. Another voice joined in; it was the toff with the pen.

'Look sir, I can vouch for him. He may not look a stalwart, but he can steer a plough, he can cut corn, which is what our Canadian cousins need.'

'Ah well Smith, smarten yourself up and be at the railway station at 7.00am on Thursday with fifteen shillings for your fare, and one pound ten shillings to start you off. The Canadians will give you a bed and board for two months. Now close your mouth and off you go!'

In a daze Bertie was walking slowly out of the room when a voice hailed him.

'I say sprog,' It was the toff again. 'Meet me at the station gates on Thursday at a quarter to seven. Smarten up, cherry flip!' And he had gone.

Slowly, very slowly and utterly bemused, Bertie Smith pushed his bike to the bakery.

In the doorway he blinked. 'Today is Tuesday Mr Merry?'

'Indeed it is.'

'I sail on the 'Earl of Strathclyde' on Friday,' he said solemnly. 'Got to lay my dabs on money by 7.00am. on Thursday.'

The baker whistled. 'Well, well you wasted no time Bertie. Canada doesn't know what it's got coming to its shores.'

'It surely doesn't Mr Merry; it's either farming or the railway.'

Mr Merry pursed his lips and widened his eyes, almost as surprised as Bertie at the swiftness of events.

'Well, off you go,' he proffered his hand, 'and come back rich . . . here's a florin to help you on your way.' The sight of the undersized sixteen-year-old brought a sigh of regret as the man hastily began mixing the next day's dough.

Six forty-five Thursday morning, saw a different boy at the station gate. By foul means, he had acquired an over-sized shirt and trousers from the Jacksons' washing-line, black boots from a pile behind the cobbler's shop, a coat from the vestry of St John's church and, while he was about it, a piece of wire and some elbow grease had opened up the Poor Box and lo and behold the Lord had helped him again: twelve silver shillings and a sixpence.

'Thank you God,' he had whispered. 'One day I'll return it, you'll see.' He muttered the same mantra crawling out from beneath his father's bed, clutching the drunken man's funeral money. He had bitten his lip quite hard at stealing this, but assured himself that he would be back before the wretched man died.

The toff now strolled up wearing a striped blazer, Oxford bags and a straw boater.

'All set?' he asked as nonchalantly as they though they were off to the seaside.

The journey to Liverpool was long enough for Bertie to learn that Cedric Bowes-Talbot was quite a colourful character, and that he had been lucky in retrieving his fountain pen.

'Some would have swiped it . . . you did not, so I guessed I owed you something sproglet? Got your cash, yes? Pants and socks in that bag, yes? Well, when we get to the docks we part company. You see, my Papa's money may have run out, but I have my return ticket, so my cabin is a couple or so decks above steerage.'

'Oh.' Bertie's face showed his disappointment and he felt even worse when Cedric cheerily said, 'Goodbye sproglet!'

The voyage would take about two weeks, but after only one night in the stinking, airless cabin that Bertie shared with half a dozen other boys, he was cursing Mr Merry's ideas for furthering his education. He was lonely. The boys were uncouth and rough, tough farmhands, who laughed at his naïveté; then he would escape to the deck into the fresh air, but with nothing but the sea to look at, he forced himself to go back to play cards or board games with the quieter of his cabin mates.

Once, taking the air in the moonlight, he almost fell over the sprawled body of a drunkard who was clutching a half-empty champagne bottle. Turning him over, Bertie was horrified to see Cedric's bloodied face, and somehow got him back to his cabin where he washed him and put him to bed without his erstwhile companion realising who he was. However, a few days later, before land was sighted, the same thing occurred again, but the next day Cedric tapped on the cabin door and peered around.

'Lawks, what a stink. Where are you Bertie?'

'Behind you.'

'Ah, let's get out of this midden hole my boy. I have to thank you for your ministrations once again.'

'Think nothing of it,' came the reply.

'Let's go up a deck. I have a suggestion for you.'

They settled themselves out of the gusting wind, yet its freshness was heaven sent. For a few moments they savoured it. With eyes raised to the hurrying clouds, Bertie asked, 'What happens when we reach Ellis Island? Shall I see you again?'

'I've been giving it some thought, Sprog.' Cedric paused, as though still thinking, and then said quietly. 'How would you like to come and work at my parents' house? We're quite . . . well , upper crust you know, and you would learn a lot about household things and speech,' he chewed his lip awhile then carried on. 'And Papa is always on the lookout for a new chauffeur.'

'What's that?'

'A driver to take Mama to her committees and Good Works, and Papa to his office. Just to get you started you know.'

'Oh, Cedric' he shook his head, 'the house stuff would be fine, but I can't drive a car!'

'Easy, old chap, easy; just put your feet down and off you go. Think about it.'

Cedric was put to work in his father's factory and Bertie, who had now changed his name to Bertram Spendleton, because he considered it would facilitate his entry through the portals of big business one day, was learning how to conduct himself in upper class company, and to drive Mr Bowes-Talbot's Lagonda motor car. At this time, he realised that he had hardly said 'goodbye' to his little sister, so he quickly wrote her a short, guarded letter.

His second letter, several months later, was more buoyant, for he told her of learning to drive and how very much he was enjoying his new life. His third came to her two years later, from the address of his serviced flat in Ottawa with news of his promotion within the newspaper industry. 'Please tell Mr Merry that I have my own column and my vocabulary is now somewhat enlarged.'

A year later, he received a reply.

'My dearest brother,

Whilst I am the happiest of sisters, that in the space of four years you have done so well, I have to tell you that our father died last month. The boys left me a while back so I am able to do little jobs to keep body and soul together.

I long to see you Bertie, your loving sister.

Florrie x

Bertie's reply was soon speeding on its way back to his sister.

Dearest Florrie, (he replied),

I shall come and get you. I have been offered a share with Cedric in this prodigious newspaper (we have a circulation 56,000!) and I move house next week;

plenty of room for you, little sister. I shall be with you
shortly.

Longing to see you,

Bertie x

When the great day arrived a year later, he was shocked at the condition of his old home and his sister's broad accent.

'We shall have to get those vowels ironed out,' he laughed, 'and some smarter clothes for such a lovely young lady.'

He left her talking excitedly to Mr Merry, while he went around the scruffy neighbourhood making amends for his earlier stealing practices, and thanking the Lord for Mr Merry's advice. Although, he reminded himself, he never did find the meaning of that word 'paucity.'

TREASURE HUNT

by Brenda Daggers

The bushes and trees in the garden shimmered yellow and green in a heat haze. Maria slumped onto a sun lounger, carefully smoothing the folds of her white cotton skirt. She closed her eyes and inhaled, breathing in the perfume of the nearby rose bushes. Reaching into her handbag she pulled out a 'scrunchy' and tucked back her coppery curls. She heard a dry click of fingers and looked up to see Steve looking down at her, brown hair flopping into his eyes. He laughed and tossed a sheet of paper into her lap.

'Come on, the clues are all there. The kids have been looking forward to the Treasure Hunt all week. Just help them follow the trail and keep an eye on them until I get back from my meeting,'

Maria sat up. She could see Lily and George scuffing around in the flowerbeds behind Steve.

'I've found a worm,' Lily called, brandishing something long and wriggly in the air.

Maria shuddered. Really, this was all too much.

'They're your kids Steve. It's not fair, that ex-wife of yours dumps them on us almost every weekend. Now we won't make the party at Gary's tonight, or the pub do tomorrow. Besides it's just too hot for a stupid game foraging around the garden looking for clues. It's not just about the children you know, what about me?'

Steve's face folded into that expression of guilt again, his smooth forehead wrinkling into a tiny frown.

'I'm really sorry sweetheart. Work's so hectic at the moment. When the pressure eases up, we'll spend some time together, just the two of us. I promise. Must rush.'

Maria propped herself on one elbow, scowling at the sight of Steve's back disappearing through the side gate of the garden, followed by the purr of his car engine and the crunch of wheels on gravel as he pulled away. She wondered how he could bear to wear a dark suit on a day like today.

She hauled herself to her feet as Lily and George plucked at her skirt, whining about the Treasure Hunt. She trudged along the twisting path towards the trees at the end of the garden, whilst the two children darted in and out of the shrubs dotting the lawn. Maria halted and scrubbed with the corner of her top at the muddy smears on her once pristine skirt.

'Oh, look what you've done to my favourite skirt with your dirty fingers. And you're making me feel hot running around like that. Come and walk nicely with me and we'll look for the treasure.'

George crawled out from under a hydrangea bush and tore off leaves and large pink globes. Shrieking with delight, he chased Lily across the lawn and stuffed them down her tee shirt. Lily's banshee screams seemed to pierce Maria's eardrums.

'Stop it, and be quiet, you naughty children,' Maria shouted as she rushed across the lawn and peeled George away from his sister.

She seated herself cross-legged on the lawn and shook away crushed leaves, petals and twigs. Lily collapsed in a sobbing heap on Maria's lap. She stroked the child's fair silky hair and saw there were green stains, as well as finger marks on her once white skirt, and a rip in the fabric near the hem. George stood nearby, a sheepish expression on his face, shuffling his feet.

'I want a lap too,' he muttered.

She held out her arms and George tumbled onto her lap, amid protests from Lily. Maria encircled both children in her arms. George leaned into her neck.

'I like doing Treasure Hunts with you. I want you to come and play with us every day for always.'

The gulping sounds of Lily's sobs gradually ceased and Maria felt the little girl's body relax like a kitten that has fallen asleep. They sat, cuddled together on the grass and Maria found she wasn't feeling cross any more. Gazing at their clear eyes and skin, soft and velvety like sun-warmed rose petals, she inhaled their sweet children's smell. She felt a stirring in her chest like the whisper of a breeze and a sudden ache of longing inside her. Clasping small, grubby hands in her own, she stood up and led the two children along the pathway towards the treasure, knowing that she had found a priceless treasure of her own.

THE CABIN

by Avril Suddaby

The cabin was below deck and when he let himself in the lower bunk was occupied. The excited chattering of several small children died away as he stood in the doorway looking around the cabin. Shocked, he gazed at the many pairs of eyes staring at him with curiosity and apprehension. His own feelings were similar as he looked back at the children and the old man reclining on the lower bunk, enjoying an impromptu picnic.

107

Could he have got the wrong cabin? No, his backpack was still on the upper bunk where he had deposited it a few hours earlier, before going up to await the ship's departure. There was so much to wonder at that he had no wish to hurry back to the stuffy cramped cabin. The deck of the rusty ageing ship was crowded - overcrowded - with people and their belongings. Some were sleeping, some chatting or playing cards, some preparing or eating food, some rigging up makeshift awnings to shelter themselves from the fierce tropical sun. He had made his way to a good vantage point, taking care not to tread inadvertently on someone. Long after the scheduled departure time the ship had at last set off, accompanied by dolphins leaping alongside. The massive fishing nets, one of Cochin's tourist attractions, passed by, and then they left the sluggish river behind; a slight breeze stirred as they came to the open sea and the journey to the Lakshadweeps had begun.

'Not to worry, sir,' said the old man. 'My grandchildren who are now keeping me company will go on deck to stay with their mothers tonight. Only Pinu, my eldest grandson, will remain in case I need assistance in the night.'

Now there was no going back. His love of islands, especially remote ones, had landed him in this situation. There was also the lure of the name. Certain place names – Samarkand, Madagascar, Timbuctoo, and now the Lakshadweeps – were all irresistible to him, siren calls enticing him to find out if the reality would live up to the romance of the name.

He had first heard of the Lakshadweeps at a small South Indian restaurant in London, where he had picked up a cheaply produced leaflet. From it he learned that the Lakshadweeps are a small group of islands in the Indian Ocean; the population is Muslim; to get there a ferry leaves twice a week from Cochin and a visa is needed to visit the islands; there were plans to develop some of the islands for tourism, catering mainly for Indian tourists, and a small airport was under construction at Bagram on the largest island. A long time before these islands would be able to compete with the Maldives, he had thought to himself.

In Cochin, on his next visit to India, he had sought the help of a local travel agent with the unlikely name of Leric Reeches, recommended to him by an Indian friend. The travel agency turned out to be a one-man outfit in a back street of Cochin. Yes, certainly sir, it was possible to go on the ferry to the Lakshadweeps. A ship would leave in four days' time and that might be sufficient time to get a visa. Yes, there was limited accommodation on the island - a few tourist cabins had been built on the beach and food was available at a nearby youth hostel which catered chiefly for Indian schoolchildren participating in a summer camp. As long as the gentleman didn't mind basic facilities, everything could be arranged. And the gentleman would want of course a cabin on the ship as it was an overnight journey, lasting twenty six hours as long as sea conditions were favourable. Unfortunately only double cabins were available so the gentleman might have to share with someone else. He had agreed to everything, left his passport with Leric Reeches and spent a few enjoyable days relaxing in Cochin until his visa was ready.

With a shrug of resignation he left the old man and his grandchildren to their picnic, and went up to the mess room. He was directed to a table where he met the other Europeans on the ship: a Dutch couple and a dapper Frenchman in the company of three exceptionally beautiful young Indian men. A meal of rice and thin vegetable curry and papadoms was served, followed by a slice of watermelon. Such was to be the unvarying diet until he was back in Cochin a week later.

When he returned to the cabin the old man and his grandson were asleep curled up together on the narrow bunk. As quietly as possible he used the primitive WC behind a hardboard partition and climbed up to his bed. He wondered if this was to be an experience where the journey itself would be better than the destination, and was soon rocked to sleep by the gentle motion of the ship.

THE FIND OF HIS LIFE

by Graham Porter

Charles Fullen sensed this could be the dig that he had
waited for all his life. Since schooldays, when he had
dreamed of becoming an archaeologist, he had
envisaged the dig that would make his name. Howard
Carter had his Tutankhamun, Basil Brown his Sutton
Hoo. Charles Fullen would have this dig at West
Smildham. He couldn't say why, but he had felt it
ever since he had taken the phone call a week earlier.

113

He had just emerged from delivering his last lecture before the Easter vacation when the faculty secretary waylaid him,

'There's a woman wants you to call her back. She's been out with her metal detector and found some coins. Wouldn't say more on the phone, but said it's important. Here's her number.'

Charles sighed. Another day, another metal detector. But a woman this time - that made a change. And, when he rang the number, the voice was excited,

'I didn't want to say more until I spoke to you personally. You see, I've found the odd coin before but never this many in one go, and I'm sure there are going to be more. I've spoken with the farmer and he says it's a field he won't need to plough just yet, so he agreed to hold off at least until I'd spoken with you. Can you meet me and come and have a look?'

She gave him the map reference and they agreed to meet the next morning. To tell the truth, Charles was more nervous than excited. His reputation for awkwardness with the opposite sex was well founded in reality. He was OK as long as he could hold a functional conversation, but got into difficulty if he ever strayed outside matters historical or archaeological. Anyway, he should be safe today. The woman had sounded quite knowledgeable and certainly kept to the subject on the telephone. He slowed the Land Rover as he reached the lane leading to the farm and was rewarded by the sight of a yellow Volkswagen exactly where she had described.

He was looking towards the VW as he stepped out of the car, consequently failing to avoid a cow pat. Not a good start. But if Rosemary Bakersfield was amused she was too polite and gracious to show it. She stepped towards him, hand outstretched, and greeted him,

'Hello, I'm Rosemary, Pleased to meet you.'

'Charles Fullen. Pleased to meet you too.'

And so, after meeting with the farmer, they had spent a morning looking around the area where the coins had been found. Charles agreed with Rosemary that it was highly likely there would be more coins to be found - and possibly more than just coins. Eventually they adjourned to a nearby pub and, over a bite of lunch, discussed the next step. Less than a week later and they were back, this time with a team of volunteer undergraduates and local enthusiasts, setting up the trappings of a dig.

Rosemary had studied Charles in the pub that day, and watched him with interest since. She knew of his reputation with women. Rosemary's similarly disastrous track record with men had a lot to do with her reasons for dropping out of a history degree four years previously. But Charles didn't know that. She looked at him again now, as they set up the dig. He had been utterly polite, friendly and charming with her from day one, and she liked him a lot.

By the beginning of May, the farmer needed his field back and they had to admit defeat. Charles and Rosemary had found a few more coins, but nothing more of interest. The local museum was displaying the new find with pride but, sadly, Charles was forced to admit that this was not to be the 'dig of his life'. And yet . . .

At breakfast, twenty years on, Rosemary spoke to Charles over his newspaper,

'Do you ever think about our first meeting, darling?'

'When I stepped out of the car into a cow pat?'

Rosemary Fullen smiled. 'That's the one'

'And I thought you hadn't noticed.'

THE SEA

by Lea Jamieson

Thud of heavy seas hitting the battered prom declares relentless might of wind and tide.

Sun bright with joy; from cliff walk the sea is edged with lace as waves cover and recede on flat, submissive sand.

A playful mood with sun catching the underside of a single wave that seems to race and break ahead of the others; translucent colours change and then they're gone confused in foam and bubble.

Clouds tinged with pink, reflect in shining wet sand and give a second sky its fame, sea echoes with rose edges to its might.

Flints add their rattle and rush as seas encroach, hump and smooth the way for other waves to come.

Tiny pebbles are sucked and spat by myriads of waves breaking one after the other; foam flies in the wind and seagulls add lament.

A tractor pulls the boat and now the cries of gulls warn others of their right for food; yellow clad fishermen move purposefully with their haul.

A dog bark disturbs the whoosh of gentle waves that nudge children's feet and touch moats of proud parent mounds.

I wonder at the mood of sea and sky. Always a gift of God's love and power.

How can one rate the beauty of the scene? It simply is and tells us to be still.

THE LAST CHRISTMAS TREE

by Stuart McCarthy

She woke me at three in the morning with a demanding elbow in the ribs and the bedside light shining full in my eyes.

'Are you awake?'

'Nnnnnn.'

Another elbow, this time in the kidneys.

'I said are you awake?'

'Nnnnnn, yesssss,' I muttered.

Another elbow.

'Are you sure?'

'Yesssss, whatsittt?'

'I want you to do something.'

'Mmmmmm,' I rolled over, arm reaching amorously across her tummy.

'Not that!' She sounded cross.

'Awwwww.'

'Now, are you awake?'

'Yes, I'm awake!' I admitted

'Good, now listen. Are you awake enough to do that?'

'Yes,' Sullen now, I prepared myself for instructions.

'Good, splendid.'

'Oh God,' I thought, that word again, 'I want to go back to sleep.' I rolled over, head turned away. She seized my chin and turned my head towards her.

'I want a Christmas tree in the front room, decorated, by the time the Dawkins arrive at twelve. Do you understand?'

Being wide awake now and with her face no more than three inches from mine I couldn't do anything else but understand.

'Yes. I'll get it in the morning,' I agreed very reluctantly.

'In the morning there might not be any left and my Christmas will be spoilt by your refusal to get me a tree. How do you think Mummy, Daddy and the Dawkins would view that?'

'But it's three in the morning?'

'So?'

'But it's Christmas Eve,' I protested.

'So?'

'But you said you didn't want a tree, too expensive you said, all those needles you said.'

'Well, you have had a Christmas bonus and you are quite capable of using the Hoover so there is no problem. We are having a tree.'

'OK, in the morning, I'll go and get one.' But even that wasn't enough for her. Another attempt to reclaim sleep, another sharp elbow in the ribs.

'How can you be so uncaring? I said I wanted a tree and I want one now. In the morning there won't be any left. So put on your clothes and go.'

Muttering silently I rose, dressed and went down into the kitchen to make a restorative cuppa.

'Now,' came the strident voice from the bedroom.

'Yes dear,' came my submissive voice from the kitchen and by the time the final echoes had died my submissive person was outside and starting the car. The bedside light flicked off and the vision of my 'beloved' wife returning to peaceful slumber triggered images of Armalite rifles.

The dashboard clock read 03.10 and the streets were deserted as I made my way to the nursery.

I arrived at the locked gates at half past three to find, to my surprise, a queue of fifteen cars, all with very crumpled people clearly seeking that last minute Christmas tree. They looked at me, the sixteenth person, and their looks were hostile. It did not take me long to work out why. Against the fence were a line of fifteen trees. I looked at my opponents in the rush for that last tree, considering which one I could 'take out' to claim my prize. They were all bigger than me except for the woman in the car in front. I tapped on the window.

'Hello, are you here to get a tree?' I asked.

'Yes,' wary, dark hair, dark eyes, thin fingers resting on the wheel.

'It's very early isn't it?'

'Yes, but he wanted one,' she agreed.

'Husband?'

'Boyfriend.' She sounded sad.

'Demanding isn't he.'

'Yeh.'

'So is mine.'

'Girlfriend?'

'Wife.'

'Oh, I see.' She looked up and met my eyes.

'What will he do if you don't get one?'

She turned her head to face me allowing the garden centre light to shine on her face. She had 'walked into a door' or 'fallen in the bathroom'; whichever it was it wasn't pretty.

'What will yours do?'

'Mental scars, she's expert,' I told her ruefully.'

'He hasn't the brains for that.'

'So he does that to you?'

'Yeh, sad ain't it?'

'Why don't you leave him?'

'Not that easy. Why don't you leave her?'

'Not that easy,' I laughed and was rewarded with a smile, I smiled back and returned to the car to catch up on lost sleep.

No sooner had I settled down and closed my eyes than there was a tap on the window. Cursing inwardly I rolled the window down. She was standing there.

'Coffee?' she asked, holding up a flask.

'Yes, thank you. Come on in.'

She came round and sat in the passenger seat. The coffee was hot and strong just how I like it. My wife never makes it like that, she says it causes too much mess and it makes me frisky.

'This is good, thanks.'

'You're welcome, I can never have it like this at home, he likes it weak, milk and three sugars.' Again, that smile.

Then we started talking. We talked non-stop for the next hour until it was almost time for the garden centre to open. We talked of physically and mentally abusive relationships, of prolonged unhappiness. We then moved onto hopes, dreams and ambitions. We only stopped when she put her hand over mine.

'Do you believe in love at first sight?' she asked, looking deep into my eyes.

'Until an hour ago, no. Now, definitely.'

'So what are we going to do?'

'Leave them.' I said decisively.

'Nowhere to go.'

'I have a flat in the centre of town.'

'Does your wife know about it?'

'No, it's the one secret I have. You could stay there and I could join you.' She heard the hope in my voice.

'I would love to. What about your marriage?'

'Just now, I don't care, but, like I said, not that easy, unless you know a good divorce lawyer.'

'As a matter of fact I do.' She was grinning now.

'And who is that?'

'Me.'

THE INNERMOST SECRET

by Shirley Buxton

Elegant silver birches now edged the eastern approach
to this ancient woodland. Mighty elms had been
destroyed by the ravages of the Dutch elm disease, but
majestic oaks still splayed their gnarled branches as a
testament to the many centuries of this forest's
existence. As Simon strode past a myriad of species
he reflected how a thousand, no probably two or even
three thousand years ago someone, just like him, had
walked beneath the branches of their ancestors.

What secrets were held in these woods? Below his feet the leaves from endless autumns decomposed to create new earth. Where storms had struck great giants to the ground, light flooded down to the forest floor, enabling regeneration. Although this forest was among one of the oldest in England, it was continually changing and that was Simon's problem. He had spent long childhood days in this forest, but now, visiting the place forty years later, he hardly recognized it.

He was looking at it all from a different angle, quite literally. The adult Simon was well over two foot higher than little Si. Today he wandered slowly, trying to absorb his surroundings, a stark contrast to the quick, darting movements of a child intent on play. In the imagination of a small boy, a fallen tree was a galleon and a low, leaf-laden branch the roof of a great hall where King Arthur commissioned the Knights of the Round Table. How could he hope to recognise his old haunts when he was looking though entirely different eyes? Many of the old trees had changed over the years, losing limbs and taking on fresh growth. Leaning against the rough bark of an ancient oak, Simon closed his eyes; trying to picture the spot that he and his friends were certain they would never forget. It was a place where they had pledged to meet in exactly ten years' time. On the twenty-first of March 1982, his army posting overseas meant he was far away in Cyprus. He had often wondered if any of the others had turned up on the assigned day. Simon had lost all contact with the gang when he'd moved with his family to London.

How he had missed his friends, not just the children but the trees as well. For Simon each tree had its own character. His favourite tree was a sweet chestnut that showered him with fruits late in September. Simon had named it Sir Galahad the Gallant. He used to press his face into the bark, whispering secrets into the patterned crevices. Trees could be trusted. Trees were strong. They were always there.

On their last day together, each of the friends had written their greatest secret on a scrap of paper. They placed the papers in an old metal box that Marty had unearthed in the hollow trunk of the 'Lightning Tree'. Sealing the box with drops from a melting candle, they each pressed their left thumb into the soft wax as a sign of commitment and loyalty to each other. With

131

great ceremony, they had lowered the box back down into the tree, vowing that it would remain there until they all met again.

Strangely it had never occurred to him before this moment that any one of the gang could have returned, retrieved and opened the box. Had the others gathered without him and read all the secrets out loud? Perhaps one of them had broken their oath and stolen his innermost secret. How awful, how humiliating, what had he written? Simon puzzled for some minutes trying to recall his words. Then a smile turned his lips, a smile that turned to laughter. He could not remember. The only way he would ever know his own innermost secret would be to find and open the box!

THE WASH

by Graham Porter

So here is the last letter I ever kept from my maiden aunt. She would have acquired that description in the days when the state of not being married, like its counterpart being married, had a different kind of significance from today. But Edie was never a 'maiden' aunt to me: just plain and simple 'Aunt Edie'. How much do I remember about her? How much did I ever know about her?

My father had one brother, who died at El Alamein in the Second World War, and two sisters. Winifred, 'Auntie Winnie', married and had three children, the only cousins on my father's side. I believe she may not have 'worked' though I know she was the organist for the local Methodist church. But it's 'Auntie Edie', or Edith to use her proper name, who comes to life through this letter.

Edith, I have since been told, dearly wished to be a nurse. But her father - a stern man, in my distant recollection - did not think this appropriate for his daughter and would not permit it. So Edith took up administrative work with London Transport. Some will recall that they ran the buses and the underground railway. In her spare time, Edie worked for the St John Ambulance Brigade so was able to live a portion of her dream, as a hobby.

The London Transport part of her life gave her the significant perk of free travel, even into retirement. So it was that Edie came from her home in south west London to visit our little family down in Sussex from time to time, just as our family began to grow. Edie got to know our three young sons in infancy, and I'm pleased to think that they have a recollection of this sweet, gentle person who was their great aunt. Whenever she came to visit, Edie would always bring a small gift for the children. Wisely, it was never anything extravagant: in fact, always a packet of 'iced fancy' biscuits - you know - the crisp little sweet ones, of varying shapes, with a layer of hard, glazed icing on them. The five of us never call them 'iced fancies'. We all know exactly what we mean when we refer to 'Auntie Edie biscuits'.

One of the sadnesses I have in looking back at the times of my childhood and into early adulthood, is that I didn't take the opportunity, as much as I might, to really get to know the person behind the name 'aunt' or 'uncle'. I hope it's easier for young people now that the labels are often dropped. Family of the previous generation - even parents - are more accessible as people. So perhaps they seem more three dimensional to their children, nephews, nieces and even grandchildren.

But I was never in any doubt of Edie's sweet and gentle nature. It took several readings of her last letter to us, before I recognised her sense of humour, and realised that my own shares much with hers. I use, without hesitation, the present tense, to say that she writes,

'So you are in Norwich at long last. Hope that you are on the way to being settled. It was a long wait! I wish you and the boys a happy and successful life . . .

. . . this notelet came with some soap that was given me at Christmas. On looking it up I find that The Wash is in Norfolk . . . '

I have never really thought of Auntie Edie as my 'maiden aunt'. I still think of her as the very best of relations.

OLD BLUE EYES

by Valerie Turner

Over the breakfast table Julia announced she was going to Berlin.

'Did you hear me?' she asked. Of course her husband had not, so she repeated her news as she poured another cup of tea, and waited.

The clock ticked, a car passed and the eight o'clock pips sounded, and she waited. She sipped slowly and waited. Then, more loudly she said, 'I shall leave on the 8am train.'

'Hm . . . what did you say?'

'That tomorrow I am going to Berlin.'

The newspaper was lowered a fraction. 'Why dear?'

'Why not?'

The paper was being folded, carefully. Julia watched, willing him to look at her.

'Shall I book a taxi or will you take me to the station?' she asked.

'Where to?'

'Oh really Eric . . . the railway station.'

'Whatever for?'

She pushed back her chair and gathering up pieces of china said angrily, 'You've not listened to a word I have said. I shall book a taxi for 7.30 tomorrow morning.'

Eric's face crumpled like a crushed paper bag. 'Where did you say you were going?'

'I am going to Berlin.'

'Berlin.'

'Oh do stop echoing me!'

'But why?'

'As I said not ten minutes ago, why not . . . ?' And she flounced out of the room to pack.

At 7.30 the next day Eric was sleeping, so she left a note:

'See you soon. Food in fridge. Don't forget to feed the cat. X Julia.'

Reading it for the umpteenth time as he wandered through empty rooms like a wraith, he noticed she had left everything in its place, with no signs of her at all: no open magazines, knitting needles or lap-top. Where had she gone? Ah, yes Berlin. Berlin? How extraordinary. They knew no one in Berlin these days. Of course they had lived there years ago . . . years ago!

He decided to take himself off to the golf club: bound to be someone there to talk it over with, he told himself.

139

Later in the day, he emailed his daughter whose reply was simple. 'Good for her!'

Thomas, their son, also surprised him. 'Good old Mum; perhaps she's got a toy-boy,'

A toy-boy? He put a stop to that facetious remark by punching the 'Off' button on his phone and sat down to cogitate.

While he was cogitating, Julia was reading through an extensive menu card.

'Julia! Julia Fawcet?'

She looked up to the bluest eyes. The man held her gaze and she thought she was drowning as surely as she had all those years ago. His arm was resting across her shoulders as it had then and he murmured as he had then: 'My dear, how lovely to see you.'

She smiled slowly, totally overwhelmed.

'May I join you?'

'Lovely.' At last, she had found her voice.' How did you know . . . ?'

'That you would stay here at the Adlon?'

She blushed, took a deep breath and then rushed on, 'It's luxurious now, very cosmopolitan . . . '

'And where we parted?' Her eyes travelled around his once-familiar face and her heart took an unbidden leap. She was pleased she had changed into the blue dress, recalling that it was his favourite colour.

'Caro said you may stay here, so I took a chance and . . . my dear you have not changed one iota!'

'Liar!' she laughed and that broke the ice.

He covered her hand with his. 'Let us order, I am starving.'

'Am I surprised?'

He winked wickedly, and then ordered champagne. And they talked and ate and talked again from a distance of so many years, so many happenings to themselves, to old friends

'So . . . where is Eric?'

'At home quietly ageing.'

'And our belle Julia?'

'Has come to my god-daughter's, your daughter's baby's Baptism.'

'A sudden, last minute decision.' He leaned towards her, gazing unblinkingly into her eyes, 'Well then, I have you all to myself tomorrow.'

'I was planning on visiting Caroline and Ben.'

'Sure, I live only five minutes walking distance from them, so we can fit them in after a hectic day together,'

'Steady, steady! I cannot impose myself...'

'Rubbish, Since Anna walked out of my life, and your god-daughter will verify this, I have become a crusty, aimless gentleman.'

Julia looked at his hand on hers a moment longer, slid it away, and then pushed back her chair.

'Richard.'

'I'm sorry, you are tired, and I'm being selfish. Come.'

He walked her to the lifts and kissed her cheek. 'Nine thirty? There's so much to see, Berlin has changed a lot since you were last here. Goodnight Julia.'

Later, in her room, she looked at her watch, and walked out to the balcony. Ten thirty! The night was young; Berlin was still loud and lively: young voices hung on the air, music, traffic. Planes were still coming into land through a cloudless sky. She hugged herself; this was going to be an interesting weekend!

Nine thirty the next morning saw her in a trim trouser suit hovering on the top step of the Adlon. Impulsively, she turned back into the reception area hurrying into one of the telephone booths.

Susanne, her daughter, picked up the phone immediately. 'Hello Mum, everything ok?'

'Absolutely. I am off sightseeing; phone your father for me; must go, dear.' And put the phone down to meet Richard. Of course, punctual as ever, his car had drawn up and he was opening a door for her.

From then onwards, Julia was transported into a magical, cosseted world that she had not inhabited for what seemed like years. Asked what she wanted to see and do, she flirtatiously said: 'Surprise me.'

He laughed and their day had begun.

He waved an arm to the left. 'As you know, the Reichstag and buildings are up there, and the Cathedral down there!'

'Yes, and is the Brothers Grimm Exhibition still on?'

He nodded. 'I think so.'

'Oh, this is lovely, Richard. Berlin was so dreary when Eric and you were stationed here and barbed wire and building sites seemed to be everywhere!'

At midday they found themselves sitting in a small restaurant with only a few diners, and the seductive music of Brahms in the background. 'I remember years ago that none of our friends liked the stodginess of German cuisine, which was why we instituted those regular Sunday roasts.' Julia remarked.

'While the children played wildly and we all argued over the Scrabble and Backgammon.'

'You may have, we women were washing up, sharing bits of news from England.'

'And then, suddenly you were gone. Did you hate a soldier's lifestyle so much?'

Julia looked down at her empty plate.

'Julia?

There was a lull in the whispered conversations and a diminishing in the volume of the sonata.

'It was another age, Richard.' She swallowed, adding, 'I am looking forward to seeing the new constructions among the old, along the River Spree. Shall we go?'

Richard got to his feet. 'Yes, there's so much to do before visiting Caroline and Ben.'

He guided her across the wide roads chatting companionably. He had always been good company, and she remembered his wit, his teasing and his ability to make her laugh. And so, the afternoon flew by. Charlottenburg was unchanged and a delight to wander around, so it was past six o'clock when

Richard deposited her at the hotel promising to be back at 7.30.

Her mind was in a whirl when at last she crawled into bed thinking of the day's events and the happiest of family evenings. She really should phone home. She would do so in a minute . . . yet within that minute she was asleep.

The insistent ringing of her mobile phone woke her with a start.

'Julia?'

'Yes?' she rubbed her eyes.

'Are you all right? It's me, Eric.'

'Of course; I'm fine.' And so unprepared was she, that though she found herself trying to focus she knew she was not succeeding

'You sound very strange. I hope they're looking after you? You will be careful, won't you? Berlin is a big city.'

'Not as big as London.' She paused. 'The baby's lovely . . . they are very happy living here.'

She looked at her watch. Heavens, it was already late! 'Eric I must get ready for the Baptism and all that follows and on Monday I'm going to re-visit Potsdam . . . remember Potsdam?'

'Yes, well, take care and give them all my very best wishes. See you soon dear?'

She slammed down the phone to prepare for another hectic day, being feted by all the relatives and friends, testing her language skills to the limit.

The church service was followed by a celebration lunch at a hotel delightfully placed among lakes and forest, a few miles south of Berlin. Julia found the over-long speeches daunting, and thought she had 'escaped' outside, unnoticed. She breathed in the aroma of the pines and was about to go and sit by the water, when a hand touched her shoulder.

'Is it too hot for you?'

She turned. 'Oh Richard! I thought I would explore a little, it is hot, but so beautiful.'

'Mind if I join you? It's a while since I've been here; I had forgotten how soporific it can be.'

The towering trees afforded a pleasing coolness, and the further they ventured into the forest, the quieter it became, until the only sound was that of their footfalls on crisp needles. At a clearing, they stopped. Richard raised his hand: a falling twig, a scuttling creature, a swish of wings and a butterfly's tremor. Immobile they listened, and then, reluctantly walked away from such tranquillity towards the lakes where human voices invaded. At first indecipherable and then, as they drew nearer, row boats, speed boats, jet-skis…such excitement, such youthful enjoyment.

'We should re-join the party Julia. Will you allow me to take you back to the Adlon?'

Once there Julia pleaded a headache, but promised him her last day and enjoyed the evening on her balcony phoning her son and daughter and writing a note of thanks to Ben, Caroline and baby Martin. She then decided to have an early night, after laying out her clothes in readiness for the morning.

Waking refreshed, she was determined to savour it, in spite of the grey mist which overlaid the city and even beyond, as Richard drove carefully out to Potsdam.

The historic house and its environs brought back thoughts of so many happy visits when her children were small.

'Come back!'

'What?' Julia shook her head. 'Sorry Richard, I was far away. You were saying?'

'Nothing so important that cannot wait. How about a spot of lunch and take the scenic route back to say good-bye to Caroline?'

'Yes, why not?'

It seemed only yesterday that she had arrived at the Adlon and was met by those twinkling blue eyes. Yet, as they sat over their last meal several hours later, each knew that their friendship had deepened. Into what, both questioned themselves? Richard looked over the rim of his glass and she met his steady gaze. He detected a sadness about her. She willed him to say nothing, and smiled, brightly.

'I shall miss all this pampering, Richard,' and as she guessed he was about to respond she rushed on,

'You have been very kind . . . I hope nothing comes to spoil our friendship.'

He bit his lip as though stemming a flow of rehearsed platitudes, 'Why should it?'

She stretched her hand to touch his, and he quickly covered it. 'Will you come again?'

A long silence ensued and after a while she murmured, 'Will you come to England?'

At Tegel airport next day, he chastely kissed her cheek as she again asked him, 'Will you?'

'Of course; I am often in England visiting friends.'

ABOUT EX-CATHEDRA, NORWICH

EX-CATHEDRA is a keen and close-knit writing group of seven members, that developed from a creative writing course studied at Norwich Cathedral in 2008 and 2009. Five of the cathedral participants are still in the group, including three who contributed to the publication, in 2010, of an anthology entitled *Voices from the Cathedral*.

Our members meet weekly, bringing a wide variety of experiences and interests. Over the past four years, as a part of our normal weekly activity, the group has produced a treasure-chest of short pieces. In 2014, a member of the group hit on the idea of using some of these stories and poems to produce an anthology specifically for those who are experiencing memory loss. We have found editing each other's work while holding this client group in our minds to be both stimulating and challenging and we hope you enjoy our efforts. Happy reading.

The seven members of Ex-Cathedra Norwich are:

Shirley Buxton. My interest in writing started when I retired from teaching. I find inspiration from past experiences, travel, grandchildren and the writings of the fourteenth century mystic, Julian of Norwich.

Brenda Daggers. I grew up in London and have enjoyed a career in Community Development work and teaching. My interests include International Folk Dance and playing musical instruments. I have one son and live with my partner near Norwich.

Lea Jamieson. I enjoyed a successful career in Midwifery. Since retirement I have focused on an allegory of a prayer journey with an interpretation, and other writing related to teaching about prayer, such as Imaginary Prayer Journeys and How to do Contemplative Prayer. I love Norfolk, living in Cromer, sailing and walking with my dog on the beach.

Stuart McCarthy. I am a retired teacher and I now divide my time between writing, storytelling and making my living on a supermarket checkout. I live in Norfolk with my wife, daughter and cat.

Graham Porter. I am a former headteacher who, in retirement, has been able to indulge my passion for putting pen to paper. Cathedral cities seem to hold a fascination for me, from my university days in Exeter to now, when my wife and I live in greater Norwich.

Avril Suddaby. I came to Norwich 10 years ago after living for 35 years in London and working as a teacher. I have a son and a daughter and four grandchildren. My interests are literature, gardening and travel.

Valerie Turner. I enjoyed a varied teaching career in Norfolk where, as a child I won several writing competitions. This talent, useful within the classroom, was later combined with my strong interest in history and travel, and has led me to writing short stories and historical novels.